Jonathan Baxter Harrison

The condition of Niagara Falls, and the measures needed to preserve them :

eight letters published in the New York evening post, the New York tribune, and

the Boston daily advertiser during the summer of 1882

Jonathan Baxter Harrison

The condition of Niagara Falls, and the measures needed to preserve them :
eight letters published in the New York evening post, the New York tribune, and the Boston daily advertiser during the summer of 1882

ISBN/EAN: 9783741173684

Manufactured in Europe, USA, Canada, Australia, Japa

Cover: Foto ©Andreas Hilbeck / pixelio.de

Manufactured and distributed by brebook publishing software
(www.brebook.com)

Jonathan Baxter Harrison

The condition of Niagara Falls, and the measures needed to preserve them :

These Letters, the result of a recent study of NIAGARA AND ITS ENVIRONMENT, are respectfully inscribed to

THE JOURNALISTS OF AMERICA,

with the conviction that if the final ruin of this scene of beauty and wonder shall be averted, that fortunate result will be brought about chiefly by the intelligence and public spirit which find expression through the newspapers of the two countries having a common interest in the subject herein presented.

Franklin Falls, New Hampshire,
October 25, 1882.

THE

CONDITION OF NIAGARA FALLS,

AND THE

MEASURES NEEDED TO PRESERVE THEM.

EIGHT LETTERS

PUBLISHED IN

THE NEW YORK EVENING POST, THE NEW YORK TRIBUNE,
AND THE BOSTON DAILY ADVERTISER,

DURING THE SUMMER OF 1882.

By J. B. HARRISON.

NEW YORK:
1882.

UNIVERSITY PRESS:
JOHN WILSON AND SON, CAMBRIDGE.

NIAGARA FALLS.

I.

[*From the New York Evening Post, Aug. 9, 1882.*]

VARIETY AND VITALITY OF THE GREAT CATARACT—
HOW TO SEE IT.

NIAGARA FALLS, N. Y., Aug. 7, 1882.

Is it worth while to report and describe truly the existing conditions at Niagara Falls? Thoughtful people find this a place of wonderful interest, of unparalleled attraction; yet some of their most vivid impressions and remembrances of the spot are eminently unsatisfactory and disagreeable. The scenery here has an absolutely exhaustless vitality. Its beauty grows upon every observer who remains long enough to recognize the truth that the spectacle upon which he gazes is never twice the same. The longer one studies the view at some points the more unwilling he is to turn away. It is like leaving a play of entrancing interest which has not yet ended. And here the play never ends. This is the great characteristic of Niagara, — its "infinite variety." There are several places in the rapids, and especially about the head of Goat Island, at each of which the changing show of the forms and motions of the water, — flinging, tossing, flying, exploding, thrown high into the air in great revolving bands and zones of crystal drops, shooting aloft in slender, vertical jets of feathery spray, swinging in wide-based, massive waves like those of the ocean, or gathered into billows which forever break and fall in curving cascades, and yet seem not to fall because they are every moment renewed, — are worth a journey across the continent to see.

FOUR SEPARATE WATERFALLS.

There is a great variety of beauty and interest even in the Falls themselves. As Luna Island divides the American Fall, making a beautiful separate cascade of the narrow stream which runs next to Goat Island, so the small island called Terrapin Rocks (on which Terrapin Tower formerly stood) cuts off a broader portion of the stream on the Canadian side of Goat Island, and makes a separate cataract there. Thus, when the spectator is on the lower end of Goat Island, there is on each side of him, first, a narrow strait or portion of the river, just large enough to form a fine fall by itself, then a small island, and farther on a great cataract, — the American Fall on one side, and the Horse-Shoe Fall on the other. These divisions of the stream, with four separate waterfalls, different in volume and environment, and so each possessing a marked individuality of character, yet so related to each other that they may be regarded as forming two great falls, and also as constituting, when all taken together, the one great cataract of Niagara, — render the scene far more beautiful and interesting than one great fall of the undivided river could possibly be; while the fact that the height of the fall is everywhere very nearly the same maintains the impression of a complete and all-encompassing unity in the central spectacle of the place. There is great variety, again, in the lines of the curves made by the descending water as it leaves the brink of the fall, as an artist would at once observe, and some of these curves are wonderfully majestic and beautiful. There are also many different curves and irregular variations in the line of the top or brow of the precipice over which the water rolls; and while for the most part the water falls sheer and free from the edge of the cliff till it strikes the stones at the bottom, there are in some places projecting rocks a little way below the top of the fall, upon which the descending stream is broken, and from which it is thrown for the rest of the way down into new lines of movement and new forms of beauty, thus adding another element of variety to the face of the cataract. In some places the stream pours with a steady roar into soundless depths of water at the foot of the precipice; in others it dashes with indescribable violence upon great masses of rock below, from which it is hurled outward with terrific force in hissing streams and spouts of spray. The color of the falling water also varies everywhere. It is of snowy, dazzling whiteness where the current is shallow above, and the descending stream consequently thin. There is a little green mingled with the white where the volume of water is somewhat greater, and in the central portions of the Great or Horse-Shoe Fall the deep, intense, solid green of the water has a wonderful vitality and beauty.

THE FRAMEWORK OF FOLIAGE.

The magnificent framework of green foliage in which this glorious spectacle of the myriad forms and shows of moving water — from the wild, gay tossing of the rapids to the solemn fall of the cataract — is set, is an essential and indispensable part of its interest and loveliness. The massive growth of trees and enveloping vine canopies on the islands and river shore give to the scene such sylvan aspects of grace, of softness and tenderness, as constitute some of the chief elements in its unspeakable charm, and some of the most forceful qualities by which it makes its eternal appeal to the heart of man. Niagara would not be what it is now if it rolled through a bare, brown desert of limestone. It is not the water — the river — alone that gives to the place its unequalled attraction, its companionless grandeur and loveliness. If the trees should be destroyed, and the shores and islands denuded of their green and living beauty, the waters might rush and leap in the rapids, and roll over the cliff into the gulf below, as now; but our sense of their sparkling gladness and gayety, and of the tenderness and passionate, eager youthfulness in the life of the scene would be gone. The sentiment of the place, and the thoughts and feelings appealed to and inspired by it, would be wholly different from what they are now; and they would necessarily be of a much lower order and of a less vital quality. The value of this scenery, as a great possession for the human spirit, a source of uplifting, vivifying inspiration for those who can receive and enjoy such influences, would be terribly, fatally impaired.

Some people do not see or feel, in any considerable degree, the spiritual charm of which I speak. They would not think of coming to Niagara for reinforcement of strength, for soothing, healing delights, or uplifting peace, or for help of any kind for the deeper needs of this life. They come hither because it is the fashion; the place lies in the round of travel, and they sit in their carriages at the top of the stairway leading down to Terrapin Rocks and look at the Great Fall for a minute and a half, and usually remark, as they pass onward, that it is a less curious and interesting spectacle than they had expected to see, and that, " on the whole," Niagara disappoints them. Of course it disappoints, and must forever disappoint, all who look at it in this foolish, hurried way. It requires time for the faculties of the human mind to be put in motion, and to respond to such a spectacle as this. Nay, it takes time even for the senses to recognize its most obvious material forms and aspects, and such persons do not give themselves time for even that. " May be I can't appreciate it as some can," they say. No ; they might, in a minute and a half, " appreciate " the burst of colored fire from a sky-rocket, and enjoy its value to the full; and they do not understand that Niagara is a spectacle of another order. Unless they can become more thoughtful, the scene here is not for them. There are other people to whom Niagara means much. It offers to those who are weary from toil of any kind, of hand or brain, or from the wearing, exhausting quality which is so marked in modern life, — it offers to all such a vital change, the relief and benefit of new scenes and new mental activities and experiences consequent upon observing them and becoming interested in them. Then, for those who will give time and opportunity for the scene to make its appeal, time for their minds to respond to its influences, there is something deeper and higher than this. There is a quickening and uplifting of the higher powers of the mind, an awakening of the imagination; the soul expands and aspires, rising to the level of a new and mighty companionship. Self-respect becomes more vital. Good things seem nearer and more real, and the nobleness and worth which but now we thought beyond attainment by us appear part of our inheritance as children of the Highest. I am not concerned to indicate the different ways in which the sentiment or spirit of the scenery, revealed through its local aspects and characteristics of infinitely varied grandeur and beauty, at last opens communication between itself and what is highest and most vital in the mind and heart of man. It is little worth while to try very hard to " enjoy " or " appreciate " Niagara. It is worth while to try to see, to become well acquainted with the form and appearance of each particular scene and part of the landscape, especially along the rapids and river shores, and about the falls as seen from above; and then, without any straining after high feeling or raptures of any kind, one is likely, by and by, to have a sense that the visit to Niagara has been a deep and vital experience, and that the place has become a real resource and possession to the soul forever. It is easy to write too much and too particularly of all this ; for such experiences and feelings, like all the higher moods and activities of the soul, have something shy and elusive about them, and it is not often best to try to describe them. And Niagara itself, in its sovereign dignity and perfection, shames and silences all effort at description or eulogy. It is to be seen, felt — not talked about. And as the weeks and months pass while I dwell here, by the very shrine of this awful beauty, this veiled and shrouded grandeur, I become more and more unwilling to write about it, and can well believe that if one remained here long, all attempts at expression regarding it would appear inappropriate and futile, and that silence would seem the only true tribute. Perhaps a great artist might feel an unappeasable longing to express his feelings upon canvas, — if, indeed, the scene is not too great to be painted.

MISUSED OPPORTUNITIES.

But I write of Niagara for two reasons : one is, that so many people, who ought to have pleasure and delight in seeing it, now come here and go away without having felt delight at all,

— go away, in fact, with feelings of disappointment and vexa-
tion, which settle at last into a decided impression and permanent remembrance of Niagara as a disagreeable place. In a
great many cases this might be wholly or in very great measure
prevented; and it is for this reason, and not at all for the sake of
any attempt at description, that I write on this subject. Most
of the people who come hither are possessed of but moderate
means to sustain the expenses of travel for pleasure or recreation,
and, in consequence, they can remain at the Falls but a short
time. Now, this is the class of persons who most need, and
should be able in greatest degree to enjoy, whatever delights
or benefits the place can minister to its visitors. The rich are
better able to take care of themselves, here as everywhere. Or,
if they do not know how to enjoy Niagara, they are able to stay
long enough to learn. But thousands come hither for whom a
day, or two days, is all the time that can be devoted to this experience. If people will manage wisely it is worth while to
travel five hundred miles to see Niagara, even if they can remain here but six hours. Most people who are here but for a
day or two throw away the larger part of their time, so limited
and precious, and lose the real opportunities of the visit almost
wholly. They go to the wrong places, and do the wrong things,
and so waste not only their time but their money. If one can
be here but six or eight hours, he should not think of using a
hack or carriage. He should walk. And any woman who can
walk two miles at home can see Niagara, can see all that is
essential or important here, without troubling a hack-driver or
being troubled by him. If women would but bring with them
a pair of comfortable shoes, already somewhat worn, and put on
clothing that is reasonably light and loose, for the day, they
could easily walk wherever it is necessary for short-time visitors
to go.

PROSPECT PARK.

The proper place to be first visited by all intelligent persons
is the point at the top of the American Fall, on the American
or village side of the river. This place is included in " Prospect
Park," and twenty-five cents is charged for admission at the
gate. It is much to be regretted that there is now no point

from which an inhabitant of our country can see Niagara Falls without the payment of a fee. But it is a fact, and visitors must, of course, accept existing conditions and conform to them. The evil is not one for which any individual persons are to be blamed. It is inseparable from the personal ownership of the land adjacent to the river at this point. The land here should have remained permanently the property of the State or of the National Government; and if the State should re-acquire the title to all the land which is essential to the scenery of Niagara, it would be a most wise and beneficent measure, and would, no doubt, tend in an appreciable degree to national advancement in civilization. The view of the American Fall from this point, of the river below, and of Goat Island and part of the Horse-Shoe Fall beyond it, is naturally the first in an ascending series which includes all that is indispensable or even very important to the visitor. There are comfortable seats in the park, the place is pleasant enough in the daytime, and the view all that can be desired from one place. But it is just here that foolish waste of time and money on the part of the short-time visitor usually begins. There is a railway down an in-clined plane through the bank to the river below; there are guides, and dressing-rooms, and waterproof suits, and all sorts of appropriate arrangements down there for creeping around, as a moist, unpleasant body, in a blinding storm of spray about the foot of the fall, and in "The Shadow of the Rock," where there is nothing of interest to be seen, and where, if there were untellable wonders, nobody could see them. Here at Niagara, where the fees are heaviest, the "sights" have least interest and value.

GOAT ISLAND.

Everybody appears to be specially interested in having you visit these places, where it is all feeing and no seeing; but the intelligent short-time visitor will say no, in a way to be under-stood, and, leaving the Park by the gate nearest the river, will walk a few rods up the stream (by the very edge of the Ameri-can Rapids) to the Goat Island Bridge. Here the fee is fifty cents. (If you are to remain for some days pay one dollar here and seventy-five cents at Prospect Park, and come and go at

pleasure without further charge.) At the island end of the
bridge take the steps up the bank to the right. A beautifully
shaded walk through the forest brings you to Luna Island, at
the top and very edge of the American Fall on that side.
When ready to proceed keep to the right from the top of the
stairway, by a pleasant path along the edge of the island, pausing at various points for characteristic views, but not pausing
for the descent to the " Cave of the Winds," where there are
more dressing-rooms, more rubber suits, more guides, more
soaking, dashing mists, etc., requiring time and money in
proportion. The walk to the Great Fall requires but a few
moments. Look at it first from the head of the stairway, then
from Terrapin Rocks (where Terrapin Tower formerly stood).

THE RAPIDS.

You must not think you have seen Niagara because you
have seen the Falls. The rapids at the head of Goat Island,
and the varied and wonderful scenery of the "Three Sisters"
at that point, — all this is indispensable. You have not seen
Niagara if you have omitted this region. It is but a few
minutes' walk again, still keeping to the right along the edge
of the island. after you leave the Great Fall. Leaving the
" Three Sisters," go directly across the carriage road, up the
steps and past the excursion or picnic building in the woods,
passing to the right of it. A broad path through the woods
leads to the end of the bridge by which you crossed to Goat
Island. Having paid your half-dollar to go to the island every
point and prospect upon it and around it is free to you. There
are no further fees.

And now, if one has followed the course here indicated,
spending, of course, as much time as he can afford at the different points of interest, and especially in the solitudes of the
islands, he may rightly feel that he has seen Niagara, or that he
has been at the right places for seeing what is essential to the
charm and wonder of the place so far as it is possible to see and
feel it in so short a time. There have been but two fees,
amounting to $1.25. If the visitor must leave now, he need
not think with much regret of what he has not seen. If he can

stay another day it would be wise to go over the same ground. But if he would see more, the next thing to be done is to cross the new suspension bridge into Canada, and go up to that side of the Great Fall ; and the next after this is the visit to the Whirlpool, some miles down the river. This last will require a carriage for most visitors. The fee on the bridge is fifty cents to go and return. The view of the Falls from the Canada side is free. A public road follows the edge of the cliff.

II.

[*From the New York Evening Post*, Aug. 14, 1882.]

THE SMALL SWINDLES AND SHAMS OF THE PLACE, AND WHAT TO DO WITH THEM.

NIAGARA FALLS, N. Y., Aug. 9, 1882.

As there is much complaint of the excessive cost of a visit to Niagara, it seemed worth while to note, as I did in my first letter from here, the fact that many persons might see all that is of ·great interest at the Falls with very little expense. What may be called the territorial concentration of the interest and value of the scenery here is most remarkable. The region which contains all that is greatly worth seeing is a very small one, and easily accessible on foot. Thus, if visitors wish to go only to places of real interest and importance, they need not waste money in either admission fees or hack-hire.

THE CURIOSITY SHOPS.

But it is said that the charges at the Indian stores are excessive, and that the principal waste of money by visitors is in purchases made at these places. This may be true, but I have little sympathy for people who complain of the extravagant prices charged at these "curiosity shops." It is true that few of the articles sold in these places are of any use whatever. Most of them are also extremely ugly, and have, therefore, no value as ornaments. The only reason for regarding them as "souvenirs of Niagara" is that they are sold here. They are not, generally, made here, or made by Indians anywhere. In some of the shops the girls tell the truth about the things they sell. I am not informed whether their candor is an injury or a benefit to the business of these places. Probably it has no perceptible effect in either way. "The prices are unreasonable, and the same things can be bought much cheaper elsewhere." Then why not buy them elsewhere? And what would be reasonable prices for things that are ugly, tawdry, and useless, vulgar in design and coarse and flimsy in workmanship? Let the people who like to "adorn" their parlors with such articles buy them, and pay whatever prices the sales-girls choose to ask. The real interest of the "Indian stores," and of their wares, is in the fact that they reflect the civilization, culture, and taste of — the purchasers. If the people of our country wished to buy tasteful and beautiful things at Niagara, doubtless such articles would be offered for sale in these stores. But why should sensible people wish to do their shopping here?

THE HACK-DRIVERS.

What is the truth about what is called the "hack nuisance"? The first thing to be noted is that each hotel keeps its own carriages, or hacks, and employs its own drivers, and these are not permitted to solicit custom. Persons in the house, desiring a carriage (and any outside as well), have but to apply at the office of the hotel. The house at which I live while here charges a dollar and a half per hour, or, for what is called "the round trip," or "going everywhere," five dollars. I think there is rarely or never any complaint regarding these drivers, or any reason for it. The men who have made the term "Niagara hack-driver" a name of terror all over the civilized world are men who are not in the employ of the hotels. They are "outsiders," or independents, who work for themselves or for different employers. They constantly solicit custom, as, I suppose, is unavoidable if they are to engage in the business at all. But it is apparent that they do not understand their business very well, and that they injure it by bad methods of work. It may be that there are some good and sensible men among them, and it is possible that people expect too much from them. Perhaps no man would long retain many high qualities if he followed their occupation. I have never had any trouble with any of the class, and have found it easy to be on friendly or comfortable terms with them, so far as is desirable; but I often observe in their dealings with strangers an element of trickiness. The information which they give to visitors is not always trustworthy. It is commonly understood here that hackmen receive commissions on admission fees paid by their passengers at some points, while for taking people to other places they receive only the carriage fares. Now it follows, under these circumstances, that, in the judgment of a hackman, the view or scenery at a particular place is especially interesting, attractive, and beautiful if his commission makes the drive thither especially profitable to him; but places which do not yield him a share of their revenues are naturally uninteresting. They are "humbugs"; they "don't amount to anything"; they are "no good." The truth seems to be — and it is what we should expect, I think, — that these men know little about the scenery, in any true sense, and care nothing about it. It would be foolish to depend upon their judgment or estimate of anything which attracts sensible people to Niagara. They do not know what is best worth seeing, but they find it most profitable, of course, to convey visitors to the most distant points. Their only interest or concern is, usually, to obtain the greatest possible amount of money for the least possible amount of work or service. There is, much of the time at least, no fixed schedule of prices. They take all they can get, and take advantage of the ignorance, inexperience, and mistakes of strangers, without scruple or limit. So far from manifesting a disposition of general courtesy and serviceableness, which is profitable in all occupations, these men often appear delighted to see anybody who does not employ them get into trouble or difficulty.

CASES IN POINT.

A day or two ago I saw a quarrel between a driver and four young men whom he had agreed to take around Goat Island for three dollars. They got in just outside of Prospect Park and rode to the entrance of the bridge leading to the island, a distance of but a few rods. Here they met some friends, or for some other reason changed their minds, and decided not to go to Goat Island. They offered the driver fifty cents, and wished to dismiss him, but he insisted on the payment of the full sum which he was to receive for the trip for which he was at first engaged, and when the young men refused, threatened to collect it by law. I have not learned whether he did so or not. A young Canadian came over a few days ago with his wife and two or three little children. At the railway station a driver agreed to take them "all around" for a dollar and a half; but the young fellow foolishly paid in advance. The hackman drove a short distance, to the first point at which the visitors left the carriage to look at something, and then went away and left them. The drivers are often wantonly offensive and uncivil to strangers. One morning recently I saw seven or eight carriages standing in line on a street leading to the river, waiting for custom. A gentleman and lady of middle age, well dressed and apparently intelligent, came up the sidewalk, engaged in quiet conversation. The first hackman began : " Gentleman, hev a kerridge this morning?—take you to the Whirlpool Rapids, 'n' all the points of int'rest—see everything f-four dollars." The gentleman answered respectfully but decidedly, as he walked on, " Thank you, I do not wish to ride." All the nearer hackmen must have heard his answer, but the next one took up the same sing-song lecture, in a little higher key, and at the end added an insolent injunction to the traveller not to let anybody make a fool of him. This was all repeated along the entire line, each driver making some insulting addition to the " cry " of the first, until two or three of them were screaming at the same time. The last one, lolling on his seat in a vulgar attitude, called out with most offensive tone and manner, " Come yere! I'll take ye and yer lady all round for nothin'." " Yes," chorused the others, " take him for nothin'—that's what he wants." I did not see the visitors again, and it is not likely that they remained long at Niagara.

BAD MANAGEMENT.

There should be some efficient supervision of this business; but there appears to be no system, no responsibility, connected with it. Nearly all old visitors to Niagara say that this nuisance—the hackmen's ubiquitous and persistent annoyance—keeps many people from coming hither, and especially that it

3

prevents many who have been here once from returning, and
remaining long enough to know and enjoy more deeply the
charm of the scenery, which seen once always beckons and
draws them hitherward again, with ever-increasing attraction.
It is common in the village to defend or excuse the hackmen by
saying that "it's the same in all other large places." But I
have been in all the large towns of our country, and I have
never seen anywhere else conduct so foolishly and stupidly
offensive on the part of hackmen. The people here say, also,
"Every man that complains has the remedy in his own hands.
Let him prosecute the drivers, and have them punished, if they
have done anything wrong." Now, however praiseworthy it
might be for a man to undertake by any means to reform the
manners of such a class as the Niagara hack-drivers, such a
work is no part of the object which one has in view in travelling for pleasure, rest, and recreation. I cannot find that there
is any public sentiment here which concerns itself in any considerable degree with these matters, or with anything else,
except the effort to obtain as much money as possible from
visitors; and even in this, as I have indicated, many people
here exhibit, in some things, a lack of foresight, of judgment,
and true public spirit, which is injurious to the interests of the
place and of their own business.

THE RIGHT REMEDY.

I would not describe this village as a bad, or "rough," place.
I only mean to say that as to its management of its own interests
as a watering-place, or summer resort, there does not seem to
be adequate wisdom, energy, or co-operation among its inhabi-
tants. An old resident here said to me yesterday, "We're a
slow-goin', sleepy old town — some nice people here, but things
goes on rather accidental like." I think it is plain that there is
not here, on the ground, such a conjunction of intelligence,
organizing powers, pecuniary resources, and efficient public
spirit, as is required for the direction of the affairs and enterprises of the local community in its relation to Niagara Falls and
the scenery about them, and to the interest of the American
people in the unequalled attractions of this scenery. The truth

is that Niagara is too great to be the possession of any local community, or of the individuals composing it. It should belong to the larger community, the State, or the nation, and be under its care as a possession of the whole people, so that this spectacle may be preserved forever unimpaired, to be to all generations the source of the highest intellectual and spiritual pleasures. It would tend greatly to benefit this town and its people if the State would purchase the land adjacent to the Falls and rapids, and the islands in the river, and assume, as would of course result, the supervision of all business that should be carried forward within these limits. And I must do the people here the justice to say that they appear very generally to understand this, and to desire the consummation of some plan which shall provide for these changes.

III.

[*From the New York Evening Post, Aug.* 17, 1882.]

CAN THEY BE SAVED?—HOW A MILLION DOLLARS COULD
BE WELL INVESTED—AN OPPORTUNITY THAT MAY BE
LOST IN TWO YEARS.

NIAGARA FALLS, N. Y., Aug. 15, 1882.

WHILE the people of this town who are interested in Niagara
Falls as a watering-place or summer resort are in a complaining
or discouraged mood, those who are engaged in manufacturing
enterprises, or who own lands which offer suitable sites for shops
and factories, are in high spirits. They lament sincerely, I
doubt not, the necessity of sacrificing Niagara, and all its beauty
and attractiveness, to business and commercial interests. They
say, "We should be glad if somebody — if the State — would
buy this property and preserve the scenery. But we cannot
afford to keep these lands merely for the sake of beauty and the
pleasure it will give to other people, when their use for manufacturing purposes will yield a large and permanent income." It is
not just to blame these persons, nor to impute sordid motives
to them, or accuse them of "vandalism" or barbarian tastes.
The men who own Goat Island, or the river front along the
American Rapids, are no more under obligation to sacrifice the
fortunes of their families in order to provide and maintain a
beautiful place of resort for the people of our country than are
the farmers of the Genesee Valley or of Southern Illinois. They
have the same right that other men have to use their property
for their own profit and advantage. These men appear to me
to possess as much public spirit as can be found anywhere
among the best people of our country. I doubt if any possible
change of owners could put this property into much better
hands. It seems to be an extremely superficial method of deal-

ing with the questions and interests involved, which leads to criticism of the land-owners and manufacturers here, — or of any other class of the people of this town, — as its chief result. It is not the vandalism or soulless greed of the people here which is imperilling Niagara, and which will soon destroy it forever unless some effectual interposition prevents the consummation of this ruin. It is really science, or the changed methods and conditions of life which the modern development of science has produced, that is sweeping away the ancient beauty of this wonderful place, and that threatens the desolation which, if we suffer it to be completed, will be matter of deepest regret to the civilized world for all coming time. Modern improvements in manufacturing appliances and methods, and in the means of transportation, have multiplied many times the value of the lands near the Falls as sites for mills, and have rendered the utilization of the immense water-power of the river imperatively necessary. If the State should purchase these lands,— as it should, in order to preserve the scenery, — the water-power could be utilized just as fully, and the mills and shops would be quite as valuable, a little farther away from the Falls.

WHAT THE LAND WOULD COST THE STATE.

The purchase by the State of territory which should include all the characteristic scenery connected with the place, all that is really valuable for its beauty in the region about the Falls, would not, in any degree or manner whatever, interfere with the development or application of the water-power of Niagara. The water can be taken from the river above the rapids, by means of canals, and carried wherever it is wanted. There is more room and there are far better sites for factories at some distance away from the Falls than can be obtained in their immediate vicinity, with just as much water and more fall — far more of both, indeed, than can ever be utilized. It is not proposed to injure any private interest in this instance in order to benefit the public. Nobody is to be forcibly or wrongfully dispossessed. All the property that is situated within the limits of the proposed reservation should be justly or even generously

paid for. It is probable that such a measure would encounter
little opposition from those who would be directly or chiefly
affected by it, — the owners of the lands and improvements ly-
ing within the region referred to as essential to the restoration
and preservation of the scenery about the Falls. It is a wonderful thing that, owing to the conformation of the ground
here, and the peculiar grouping of the various objects or places
of chief interest, the beauty of the scenery can be restored, and
its value retained forever unimpaired, by the appropriation of
so small a region or territory for the purposes of a reservation.
Goat Island and the smaller islands near it, all taken together,
contain between sixty and seventy acres. The other islands,
though very beautiful, are, most of them, very small. Then, on
the American side of the river, the extent of ground which
would have to be purchased, according to the best plan that has
been proposed for a reservation, would be only about seventy-
seven acres. In 1879, Mr. James I. Gardner, director of the
New York State Survey, and Mr. Frederick Law Olmsted re-
ported to the Legislature that "on the main shore, by the
removal of seven good buildings and ten of little value, the
river front of Niagara village may be cleared from Port Day to
Upper Suspension Bridge, giving a belt of public land a mile
long and widening from one hundred feet at the head of the
rapids to eight hundred feet broad at the Falls, where most
room is needed for visitors." The "improvements" on this
belt are about the same now as when these gentlemen examined the ground and made their admirable and interesting
report. The probable cost of establishing the proposed reservation has been estimated at about $1,000,000. This would be
a small sum for the State of New York to invest in securing so
great a possession and benefit to her people forever. To restore
the river shore along the American Rapids to its pristine beauty
would be a real triumph of civilization, and a notable instance
of the employment of the noble art of landscape gardening in
successful co-operation with nature for the attainment of the
highest and most beneficent ends. Some of the eldest among
my readers can recall the sylvan loveliness and wildness of this
shore when it was yet, in great part at least, undespoiled and

undisfigured. Now it is difficult to imagine, if one has not seen it, so much ugliness, untidiness, and, in places, squalor, as one sees on parts of this small belt of land. There are spots that recall the dismal, hopelessly littered and neglected look of the suburbs of some towns in Arkansas. (My readers must say *Arkansaw*, or they will not feel the full force of this comparison.)

THE WORK OF DISFIGUREMENT.

Let me quote again from the special report of the Commissioners of the State Survey on the Preservation of the Scenery at Niagara Falls : —

"Half-way between Goat Island and the American side of the river is Bath Island, whose position in the middle of these rapids must have made it a fascinating place in early days. In an evil hour it entered into some man's mind to start a paper-mill there, — small at first, but extending year by year, till, in place of graceful woods, the ground is covered with unsightly sheds and buildings, and the rapids above are disfigured by wing-dams and ice-barriers; the whole group forming a shocking contrast to the natural scenery. This paper-mill is, however, only one among the many abominations which mar the beauty of the American Rapids. Their eastern bank was once rich in verdure, and overhung with stately trees. In place of the pebbly shore, the graceful ferns, and trailing vines of former days, one now sees a blank stone wall with sewer-like openings, through which tail-races discharge; some timber crib-work, bearing in capitals a foot high the inscription, 'Parker's Hair Balsam;' then, further up stream, more walls and wing-dams. Overlooking this disfigured river brink stands an unsightly rank of buildings in all stages of preservation and decay; small 'hotels,' mills, carpenter shops, stables, 'bazaars,' ice-houses, laundries with clothes hanging out to dry, bath-houses, large, glaring white hotels, and an indescribable assortment of miscellaneous rookeries, fences, and patent-medicine signs, which add an element of ruin and confusion to the impression of solid ugliness given by the better class of buildings. And all this is the background to one of the grandest spectacles in the world, — the rapids of a mighty torrent writhing and foaming in the fury of its downward rush. Is it any wonder that visitors do not desire to remain long in the presence of such discords, but, when the first feeling of curiosity is satisfied, hasten away? In looking at the Falls from Goat Island or the Canada side, one cannot help seeing these rows of buildings which line the village

shore of the river.   Only one spot invites the eye to rest on its green
trees.   This is Prospect Park, at the east end of the American Falls.
But even here the hand of the progressive owner has torn away the
shrubs and rich masses of woodbine that clustered along the edge of
the precipice, and in their place are seen walls and structures sup-
posed to be for the safety and entertainment of travellers.   The Falls
themselves man cannot touch; but he is fast destroying their beautiful frame of foliage, and throwing around them an artificial setting of
manufactories and bazaars that rouse in the intelligent visitor deep
feelings of regret, and even of resentment."

It will be observed that, in all that I write of this subject,
the point of view is the conviction that for all the disfigurement and destruction of the lovely scenery here that has yet
taken place, little if any blame rests upon the owners of the
land, or, indeed, upon anybody; or, if anybody is really culpable, the fact is a barren one, and nothing can come of insisting
upon it.   The gradual, ever-advancing, total ruin of Niagara is
inevitable, if the private, personal ownership of the lands under
consideration is to continue.   Under no possible circumstances
could this ruin be prevented and the permanent preservation of
the scenery be secured, without the extinguishment of the titles
by which the ownership of these lands is now vested in individuals, and the conversion of this small territory into a public
domain and trust.   There are various things worth attention
here, in their relations to national civilization and the wisdom
and happiness of the American people; but when regarded intelligently and seriously, they all converge to this conclusion.

GOAT ISLAND TO BE SOLD.

I am informed that the youngest heir to the estate of which
Goat Island is a part will be of age in less than two years from
this time, and that steps will then at once be taken for the sale
of this property.   We already owe much to the Porter family
for having so long resisted all efforts to purchase the island for
purposes of perversion and destruction, but their guardianship
over this magnificent piece of primeval forest cannot be much
longer continued.   The sale of the island will soon become a
necessity.   There was much talk here a few years ago, as well

as in Buffalo and in New York City, of building a great summer hotel on the island, with bowling-alleys, a rifle range, and various means of amusement for visitors. But solid, practical business judgment is now in the ascendant here, and people begin to see pretty clearly that, as the woods are cut away, and the scenery disfigured and ruined, the number of visitors to Niagara diminishes; and that if Goat Island were dismantled of its beautiful trees, and its ruin completed by the erection of a mammoth hotel and appliances for popular amusement, the real attractions of the place would be destroyed, and nobody would come to be entertained or amused. The value of hotel property here is likely to suffer serious decline unless something effective is done to save Niagara, and it is not probable that new investments of any great magnitude will be made in enterprises of this class. When Goat Island is sold, if it does not become the property of the State, it is likely to be purchased for manufacturing purposes. Regarded without reference to its value for the high uses of beauty, or its worth to the intellectual and spiritual side of man's nature, the island furnishes a convenient site for the greatest factory in the world. Once devoted to industrial uses, there would be no reason whatever why it should not be completely covered with mills and shops and the canals and race-ways supplying them with water. In my first letter I observed that Niagara would not be what it is now if it rolled through a bare, brown desert of stone; let us extend the terms of the statement a little, and say that it will not help the matter in the least, so far as beauty is concerned, if we pile the stone into gigantic mills and manufactories.

IV.

[*From the New York Evening Post, Aug.* 29, 1882.]

THE CHEAP EXCURSIONS — CHARACTER AND MANNERS OF
THE EXCURSIONISTS — IMPENDING RUIN OF NIAGARA —
THE DUTY OF THE STATE.

NIAGARA FALLS, N. Y., Aug. 25, 1882.

I HAVE been engaged for several weeks this summer in study-
ing American civilization and manners as they are observable
in the appearance and deportment of visitors and excursionists
at Niagara Falls. It has for some years been the fashion to
lament the growth, to the enormous proportions they have
attained, of cheap excursions to the Falls. They now bring
people hither from as far away as the banks of the Mississippi,
in great companies of neighbors and friends travelling together,
and return them safely to their homes, at so small a cost that, as
a matter of fact, nearly everybody who lives in the prosperous
" old West," or great interior agricultural region of our country,
can now afford to come to Niagara. The fact that many tens
of thousands of these people from the farms and the rural towns
do come each summer is often spoken of as something to be
regretted as one of the most disagreeable features of the situation at Niagara. It is said that the presence of the excursionists keeps the better class of visitors from coming hither ; that
because they come in such numbers for their brief stay of a day,
or a day and night, many persons of wealth, who would tarry
for weeks or months at the great hotels, now remain away
altogether, or, if they come at all, make their sojourning but
little more protracted than that of the excursionists. This is
the view of some hotel-keepers, and of some persons who write
pleasant and entertaining letters from the Falls to the news-

papers. It is undoubtedly true that the number of visitors who remain for a considerable time has greatly diminished within a few years, and that this is, in various ways, to many persons, a very serious matter. But, after much observation of the facts and conditions of the situation here, I incline to the opinion that we must look in other directions for the principal causes of this diminution. I do not think that many people who wish to come here are kept away by the excursionists. Why should they be? I have seen nearly every excursion that has come to Niagara this summer, and have gone about the place with the people, observing their proceedings and characteristics as thoroughly as possible. They are often described as "rough people," as "crowds of free-and-easy men and women," and their presence here is spoken of as "offensive," and as one of the "vulgarities" of the place.

Much of this seems to me rather a European than an American view of the matter. Among a hundred thousand people here this summer I have seen little rudeness or coarseness of any kind. There has not been a noisy or boisterous company in Prospect Park, where all excursionists go. The records of the magistrate's court in the village show that there is very little more disorder here than if nobody came to see the Falls. A very great proportion — by far the larger part — of the people who have come here in excursions this summer were evidently well-behaved and reputable members of their communities at home. When we remember that almost every excursion party is largely composed of families travelling together, we can understand, what I am sure is the fact, that the behavior of the great mass of excursionists at Niagara is about the same as the behavior of the great mass of the well-to-do, comfortable, respectable people of this country when they are at home. The worst thing I have observed in the conduct or manners of visitors of this class is their habit of walking about in the town five or six abreast, so as to crowd people into the gutters from even the very broad sidewalks of the village. A company of young men from the country seemed much surprised when I refused to turn out, and thus halted the entire band of them as they were walking with "locked arms." I explained that the people of the town were, equally with themselves, entitled to the use of the sidewalk. They apologized, and broke into couples. Their fault probably resulted from thoughtlessness.

The excursionists are criticised for dancing boisterously within sight of the cataract and within hearing of its solemn roar. As to boisterous dancing, I can only say that I have each week attended the "hops" at the principal hotels, which are conducted by the guests, people of the highest social position and character, and have also looked on at all the dances in Prospect Park, and there were only very slight differences observable in the manners of the people at the different entertainments. Young people cannot sit in silence gazing at the Falls, through all of a long summer day, thinking of æsthetic sublimities, or communing with the Absolute and Infinite. I saw one excursion which was largely made up of school-teachers from Ohio, Indiana, and Illinois. I talked with some of these, and found that a good many of them come every year. I was interested in learning how they regarded the place and its attractions and opportunities. One woman who is growing old in teaching in the same country neighborhood in Western Ohio said she had been here every year since the cheap excursions were arranged. "It is a great blessing to many teachers," she went on, "and to other people, of course, that they can come here at such slight expense. If we had to pay the regular fare we could not come at all. This is my one holiday for the year, the only indulgence I can afford, and though I live so far away, Niagara is a great deal to me. I do not see how I could live without it." This all seemed reasonable enough, but I was a little surprised when she said that she read everything she saw relating to Niagara. I found that she had followed very intelligently the newspaper discussions regarding the progressive destruction of the scenery here, and the need of some interposition to save what remains. She said, "The newspapers say that the colored lights are thrown on the Falls to please us excursionists, but they need take no such pains for us. I am sure all intelligent people feel disgusted and indignant at the sight."

LOCAL OFFENCES.

I think we should rejoice that it is possible for the people of
our country to come in such multitudes and from so great dis-
tances to enjoy this wonderful spectacle of Niagara ; and if they
could be left to the natural influences of the scenery, all would
be well. The excursionists do not bring with them the vulgarities and impertinences which make the place disagreeable to
intelligent persons. These offences against good taste are es-
tablished and maintained here in the rivalry of the proprietors
of the different points of approach to the river. This competi-
tion develops more and more sensational and vulgar efforts to
attract sight-seers. Such shows help to corrupt the public
taste, doubtless, but it is not fair to say that the popular taste
produces or requires them. They all result from the private
ownership of the land at all the points from which the river or
the Falls can be seen, and no essential reform or improvement
in these repects is possible while this continues.

SHOP-GIRLS AND CUSTOMERS.

For some of the " annoyances " of which visitors to Niagara
complain they are themselves often chiefly responsible. Thus
the young women at the " Indian stores " and bazaars are blamed
for inviting passers-by to come inside. But they do so because
strangers stop at the tables or show-cases outside and examine
or handle the goods. If people will proceed directly upon their
errands, and not themselves invite the attentions of the shop-
girls, I think they will never be asked to enter a shop or to buy
anything. But most visitors appear to regard the shops as
museums, or places for the free exhibition of " curiosities," merely
for the entertainment of strangers, and many, even of the " carriage people," manifest greater interest in looking at the queer
goods in the bazaars than in seeing the Falls, or any part of the
wonderful scenery here. A few evenings ago I was observing
the movements and characteristics of a crowd of people in one
of the largest of these places, when a well-dressed young man
entered and began a tour of the store. One of the young women
advanced, and courteously asked if he wished to look at any

particular class of goods. She accompanied him to every show-case in the room, exhibiting the goods, and replying to his constant questioning. He occupied more than half an hour in this inspection, and bought nothing; and I noted, as he passed me in going out, that he did not even thank the young woman, or in any way acknowledge the patient courtesy of which he had been the object. After much observation in these places it seems to me not entirely just to apply the term "low" to the shop-girls here. Most of them live here, and many are members of the churches of the village, and are regarded by those who have the best opportunities for knowing them as young women of good character. No one who comes hither to enjoy the scenery need be in fear of annoyance at the hands of the shop-girls.

GOOD AND BAD MANNERS.

Most of the impressions derived from my observation of American manners, character, and civilization at Niagara, are favorable and encouraging rather than otherwise. There are some exceptions, of course. There is often room for considerable improvement in manners. I saw in Prospect Park a coarse fellow, with grimy hands and clothing, serving a party of young girls with ice-cream while he smoked a cheap cigar and puffed the smoke in their faces. The crowds are, in general, wonderfully well-behaved. One thing, which is, as I am told, in large degree peculiar to America, is most gratifying here and elsewhere, — that is, the behavior of young men and women when together. It is somewhat common of late to hear our customs and methods of social life in this particular respect compared with those of European countries in a manner unfavorable to our habits and character. But the great mass of American young men care more for the society, or "company," of the young women of their acquaintance than they do for lascivious pleasures, and the young women are far more secure from evil than they would be if European ideas of the relations between the sexes were generally adopted by our people.

THE REAL CAUSE OF NIAGARA'S DECLINE.

I see two classes of facts at Niagara. There is abundant proof that there is a large class or number of people in our country who feel the charm and worth of beautiful scenery, and who find great delight and refreshment in the natural loveliness and grandeur peculiar to this place. Each year people of this class are less and less inclined to visit Niagara, and their aversion is due to the increasing disfigurement and destruction of the scenery. The desolation and ugliness through which one must now pass to reach Goat Island, and all the best places from which to see the Falls, repel far more of the better class of visitors than are kept away by the presence of the excursionists. It may, or may not, be strange, but it appears to be true, that the people who are interested in "commercial enterprises" near the Falls have no feeling for beauty, and some of them appear to have a morbid and horrible delight in littered and disorderly ugliness. This belongs to the saddening, discouraging class of facts respecting our national character and feeling. We have multitudes of people who cut and destroy the finest trees and shrubs about the Falls (the excursionists are not worse than other visitors), and who cut up and pull to pieces, whenever it is possible, the seats and railings provided for their pleasure and safety. At many points on Goat Island from which good views can be obtained comfortable seats furnish opportunity for rest. Each one must be constructed of heavy timber, and have an iron rod attached, which holds it to a broad foot, or anchor, many feet underground, or it would be torn up and thrown into the river. Well-dressed " ladies " stand by and applaud while the "gentlemen" of their party do these things. In what schools, Sunday schools, and churches, are these people educated, and what is the nature of the instruction by which their character is formed ?

The danger of complete extinction, which now menaces all Niagara's natural loveliness, arises primarily from the fact that we have, in our national character, so little feeling or regard for beauty, or for anything beautiful. Those who find refreshment, delight, and spiritual sustenance in beauty of any kind are comparatively so few that they have little influence, and they do not constitute a class; they have no voice, no aim, no co-operation. Doubtless, if even the few cared enough for such spiritual verities, they would find some means for the propagation of their faith in them. The masses in our well-to-do democracy feel no discomfort from hideous ugliness and vulgarity in the objects and scenery around them at home. Our wealthy manufacturers buy costly pictures which they do not understand, while the village sites which they own, and the grounds around their mills and tenement-houses, are arid wastes of litter, filth, and squalor. Even dealers in flower-seeds in our country choose to advertise their business by means of repulsive pictures. There is an enormous popular appetite for things grotesque, monstrous, and vulgar, for thorough, debasing ugliness. Our young people are being taught to enjoy comic lives of the world's saints and heroes. We behold, without remonstrance or regret, the destruction of sylvan scenery of exquisite loveliness along the streams of the Adirondack region, wrought for the sake of making those wildwood river-channels navigable for vulgar and wholly unnecessary little steamboats. (They are vulgar because they are wholly unnecessary and out of place.)

I observe that it is common to say of the Falls that they have an eternal beauty which man cannot destroy, and that whatever may be done by capitalists and manufacturers, Niagara will be "a joy forever," etc. The truth is that manufacturers and capitalists can wholly destroy the beauty of the Falls, and they are likely to do so, and to make the place one in which no human being can ever feel joy again. Another misconception is the notion that the people here have so impaired their property, and lowered its value, that they are now anxious to have the State, or the country, take it off their hands, paying them a good price for it, and that they are likely, by and by, to "beg to sell out." Nothing could be farther from the truth. The value of the land here is increasing year by year, and what threatens the final destruction of Niagara is the fact that the very land which is essential to the beauty here has become so valuable for manufacturing purposes that the present owners cannot afford to keep it for the sake of the scenery.

These errors should be corrected, and should not hereafter be repeated by journals of character and influence.

If the people of the State of New York shall decree the purchase and preservation of Niagara, it will be an important step in its bearing upon national character and civilization. It will help to prepare us for wiser treatment of some matters of serious moment than we have hitherto been able to give them.

5

V.

[*From the Boston Advertiser, Aug.* 3, 1882.]

THE RESIDENTS DESPONDENT AT THE DEARTH OF VISIT-
ORS — THE CAUSES WHICH HAVE BROUGHT THE FALLS
INTO DISREPUTE — A PRACTICAL REMEDY SUGGESTED.

NIAGARA FALLS, N. Y., July 29, 1882.

THE people of the town are despondent this summer. The
number of visitors to the Falls is much less than usual, and
some of the best hotels are not nearly half full. As most of
the people of the place are largely or wholly dependent on its
character as a summer resort or watering-place for the means of
subsistence, they have reason for feeling, as they express it,
"mighty blue." It has, for the most part, been a cool summer
here; but when I refer to this fact, and predict a rush of visitors
on account of the warmer weather which has recently begun,
the older residents shake their heads, and say, "Yes, we hope
so; but things have changed. Niagara will never be what it
has been unless something is done." This opinion seems to be
well founded. Men who have always been connected with
"the Falls business" say frankly that people do not like to
come here so well as formerly; that the special attractions and
points of interest have been multiplied beyond reason; that
there are too many hackmen, too many "Indian stores," too
many hotels. All this is probably true.

I have met here this summer, as at the time of other visits, a
good many elderly gentlemen who, remembering their enjoyment here "in the old times," as they phrase it, come back now
with their children and grandchildren, to enjoy the young people's surprise at their first vision of the grandeur and beauty
peculiar to the place. But the young people wonder that the

elders should have seen so much here, and the elders themselves are disappointed and indignant. They lament the loss of all the wildness from the American side of the river, the all-pervading impertinence of the hackmen, the perpetual solicitation of patronage by various classes of people, and the horrible vulgarity of the colored electric lights. Many of them say that twenty-five years ago it was pleasant to remain here for several weeks, but now "one day and two nights is enough ; " and the younger folk are equally ready to seek other scenes after this brief stay.

I have also talked with some business men from New York City, from Buffalo and Rochester, who say that Niagara is really already destroyed, — the old or true Niagara, — that is, that its character as a place appealing to the heart and imagination by its wondrous beauty and grandeur has already been taken from it, and that, considering the temper and character of the American people, and the tendencies of the modern world, this character can never be restored to it. They say, "The State ought, of course, to buy it and preserve it forever, but it will not; or the National Government ought to interfere to stop this huddling of factories and dung-heaps right around the Falls. Something — anything — ought to be done, but nothing will be. We shall make cloth and paper, flour and beer and whiskey, with this unlimited power, and the people who like to look at beautiful things must go somewhere where we can't build mills." "No," said one of the company, after remarks like these, "the artistic people can go over yonder to the art gallery in the park."

Let us consider some of the matters here suggested. Recognizing as I do the unequalled value of Niagara as a source or means of strength, refreshment, and happiness for millions of men and women, and of elevation and beauty in our national character, and feeling most deeply interested in the effort to restore and preserve it for these high uses, I am still of the opinion that if the ground about the Falls were really needed for cotton and paper mills, or any other necessary and productive human industries, it would be right to take it and appropriate and occupy it for these objects. We shall have a vast and crowded population in this part of our country before any great time has elapsed, and we are preparing conditions here in America under which the mass of men must, in large degree, live for bread for themselves, and little beyond. Whenever there is a real conflict or antagonism between economic, business or industrial interests on the one hand, and ideal or æsthetic considerations on the other, the latter must give way, and rightly, because they are secondary or subordinate when compared with the necessities of physical subsistence.

But in this case of Niagara Falls, and the question of its preservation or destruction, there is really no such antagonism between practical business interests and those which are ideal and spiritual. There is no good reason for "huddling factories around the Falls,"—no need of it whatever. I think it the idlest thing in the world for anybody who desires the preservation of the scenery here for ideal and spiritual uses to decry or contemn the commercial spirit or business energy of our time, or to lament its application to this particular object,—the utilization of the water-power of Niagara for manufacturing purposes. He is a poor, shallow poet or artist who can see only the poetic or artistic side of things. The mass of men must always toil. Infinite drudgery is required to sustain human life under the conditions of civilized society. Millions of men must labor — must labor honestly, nobly, and happily — that one great poet may sing their life, or one man of divine genius paint a picture of immortal power and beauty.

Build the factories, then, and let Niagara turn their wheels. But where shall the factories stand? It would be a most insane and outrageous thing to place them here, amid these scenes unparalleled on the planet. It would be a wholly wanton sacrilege, a profanation unusually culpable, because entirely unnecessary. The Niagara River above the Falls lies so high above all the country below them that the water can be taken almost anywhere away from the river channel. Only a very small region immediately adjacent to the cataract and the rapids, with the islands in the river, — this is all that is required to make this place, or keep it what nature made it, a place endowed, as no other place on the globe is endowed, with qualities suited to refresh, elevate, and gladden the mind and heart of civilized man forever. It is a sad error and wrong that this small territory, which includes all that is essential to Niagara, — all its wild grace and ineffable charm, — should be held by any private or individual ownership. It should be the property of the State, the possession of the people, and should be held in trust and cared for by the government. All its wealth of beauty and of high uses should be accessible to the poorest children of toil who may, by wise forethought or self-denying frugality, save from the price of their labor the means for a pilgrimage to this shrine of ideal and spiritual reality.

For we must have something besides factories, and turbine wheels, and supply and demand, and daily toil for daily bread, even for the toiler himself, so that he may have " a daily beauty in his life," to use Shakespeare's phrase. You see, gentlemen capitalists and manufacturers, the laborer must toil *happily*, or you may all come to grief together, and capital must supply and maintain the conditions of beauty and happiness for him. Labor, directed and ennobled by the ideal, moral, or spiritual element, creates everything; but a democratic civilization, based on the labor of a class of serfs of the mine and the mill, whose toil is unwilling, degraded, and faithless, would not be likely to endure long in a world where the deepest meaning of everything is moral.

Let us have a great city of factories, sustained by the waterpower of Niagara. We are destined to have it. It is entirely right that this immense endowment of mechanical forces for the use of mankind should be employed to supply their physical wants. Only let us have the mills a little at one side; not just here at the Falls. There are quite as good and even better sites for them a little farther away. Put them far enough back from the Falls and the rapids to give room for a screen of trees between, — far enough for the distance to soften the clangor of steam whistles, so that on Sunday, or (as I observe that many laborers in New England mills have to work on Sunday) at least on the Fourth of July, the toiler of the factory may come to the Falls, and, looking upon their grandeur and noble purity, undefiled by tawdry electric lights, or watching the wild play of the rapids, or wandering amid the solitudes of "the forest primeval" on Goat Island, may feel that he has a soul, and is not a mere driven beast of burden, and that he has a country which cares for him as one of the great brotherhood of her children.

All this may be realized if the plan for the purchase by the State of the land immediately contiguous to the Falls is taken up and carried forward by the men foremost for business ability, intelligence, and patriotism in the State of New York. But there is need for earnest and prompt action on their part. Already there are mills and factories of various kinds where no factory or shop should ever have been built. Some of these are being enlarged. One beautiful island has been entirely destroyed for all purposes of beauty of scenery. Others are threatened by the same destiny. The river bank along the whole extent of the American rapids has been denuded of the beautiful forest growth of trees and vines which formerly gave it such loveliness, and is now disfigured by a long array of unsightly buildings, — mills, sheds, houses, barns, etc.

A strip of land about a hundred feet wide here, broadening to some eight hundred or a thousand feet in width around the American side of the Falls, — this, with Goat Island and the other islands in the river, forms the extent of the proposed reservation. Many people here appear eager to have the State obtain control of the Falls, believing that such a change would be of great benefit to all the interests of the town. Knowing that many sons of the Old Bay State are now business men in the city and State of New York, I send this notice of affairs here to the readers of the "Advertiser."

VI.

[*From the New York Tribune, Aug.* 23, 1882.]

AN INLAND RESORT.

NIAGARA FALLS: THEIR TRUE INFLUENCE, POWER, AND
SPIRIT, AND THEIR IMPENDING RUIN.

NIAGARA FALLS, N. Y., Aug. 21, 1882.

ONE of the positions where one seems to approach nearest to
the very seat and throne of the grandeur of this place is at the
end of the bridge or platform at the west side of Goat Island,
which extends for some distance over the waters of the Great
or Horseshoe Fall. This affords the most perfect view of the
central portions of the great cataract. It is perhaps the place
at which one should linger longest. The soul of Niagara is
there, visible yet elusive, revealed fitfully, with features and
elements which are essential to natural scenes of the very highest
order of interest and wonderfulness. The awful beauty of the
water in the deeper portions of the current, as it rolls over the
brow of the precipice ; its strange and indescribably impressive
color; the apparent slowness of its calm motion in the first few
yards of its downward course, which somehow seems an image
or actual revelation of eternity, — these things make one feel as
if he ought not to come to the place too often, as if on some
days, or in some moods, he ought not to come at all.

Then there is another feature of marvellous beauty and attractive, engaging interest here. I can only indicate, not describe, its character. From the centre of the Great Fall, or
extreme upper part of the curve (which has of late years been
cut so far back by the current that it now bears little real resem-

blance to the form of a horseshoe), there arises a peculiar dis-
play of mist, or white vapor, produced by the concussion of the
water against the rocks below. If this were constant in character, or of uniform appearance, it might be beautiful, perhaps ;
but it could not have the strange power of fascination which it
now possesses, — the power to hold one watching for hours its
fitful, irregular, always startling returns, and to beckon and
draw him back from distant lands to seek the same spot and
yield himself again to the spell. From the gulf below, at this
heart of the Great Fall, there arises now and then what may be
described as a great upward explosion of the mist, reminding
one of the play of volcanic forces or the spouting of an enormous geyser. A great column of white vapor is suddenly shot
upward, far above the top of the fall. The explosive force still
seems to be at play in the heart of it as it rises, and with a
swift flashing motion the top of the column expands on every
side, forming a mighty dome, which for the time of one quick
glance sometimes looks like solid marble, but is in a moment all
unbuilt and dissolved again. At other times the freakish wind
leaps at the column as it reaches its greatest height, and drives
and scatters it all abroad in strange forms, that seem almost to
have meaning and purpose.

A little farther east than this is a place at which slender
jets of water and spray are projected perpendicularly to a great
height. Sometimes a great number of these appear, springing
upward, side by side, slightly unequal in altitude, and looking,
"for one transcendent moment," just before they begin to waver
and sink, not domelike, but like a great cluster of delicate Gothic
spires or pinnacles. The background of the picture of which
these mist projections and creations form the centre, is, on the
right, the face of the western side of the Great Fall; on the
left it is the breadth of the river above, filled from shore to
shore, and to the sky-line in the distance, by the glad, eager
dance, and hurrying, wanton rush of the rapids. Here, if anywhere, one can forget the burden of care, of "greetings where
no kindness is," and the inevitable vulgarities of the struggle
for the survival of the strongest. It seems as if one had been
admitted to the primal home of the forces which made the

world and can unmake it again, and had found them in full
play.

Another scene of perfect, unsurpassable grace and power,
displayed in forms wholly unlike those I have just described, is
the region at the head of Goat Island, including the many small
islands there, and the swift, arrowy currents dividing them,
with the wide expanse of plunging, rock-tormented water beyond. In places the river is as rough as a storm-swept sea.
But the manifestation of power here is not greater than that of
beauty. The scene is full of grace and delicacy, of influences
most potent to soothe and gladden and refresh the spirit of
man. It is fitted, in a remarkable degree, to inspire, "vital
feelings of delight." This upper end of Goat Island is probably,
for most people, the best of Niagara. It is not likely that there
is anywhere else on the globe so much beauty and interest of
the very highest character and variety, displayed in a region so
small as this. All the conditions appear to be perfect, and for
the higher uses of the human spirit the scenery is of inestimable
worth. If, now, people could be brought to think a little, so as
to understand what is most essential in the conditions and elements which constitute this perfect charm and loveliness, it
would be well for them; they would regard their possession in
this unparalleled landscape with deep and passionate delight,
instead of the languid, superficial interest, scarcely above indifference, with which they now usually think of it, at least
when they are not here. What then is it that gives its peculiar
potency to the appeal which nature here makes to the heart
and imagination of man? The water — the river — is not the
whole of it. This alone, or in association with masses of bare
rock of the same size and form with the islands, would not be
especially beautiful. The spiritual power and grace of the
scene, its peculiar and delicate charm and delightfulness, would
be wholly destroyed if the trees and shrubs and vines which
now cover the islands with the glory of their foliage were removed. There is a natural congruity and harmony between
the forms and appearances of swiftly tossing waters, with their
bright, glancing rush and passionate dance, and the forms of
the native vegetation as nature shapes them. One soul of

grandeur and beauty pervades these gigantic trees (which stood
here, extending their boughs abroad in the sweet air and light,
before our nation's history began), with the umbrageous thickets
and festooning vines which crowd around their feet, and the
broad and generous waters which nourish and sustain them all.
The river, with the loveliness of its dividing flow, and the
mighty trees, with their masses of draping foliage, belong together, and together they build and perpetuate the surpassing
beauty and wonder of the scene, creating it anew each year
forever. If the trees were removed, the scenery here, with all
its peculiar interest and beauty, would be entirely and irre-
trievably ruined.

The trees with their foliage form green barriers and leafy
screens, cool arbors and entrancing vistas, and the imagination
is quickened and exalted as the eye is caught by the white
gleam of the free streams flashing through the natural, irregular
openings in the green foliage. It is all beautiful here at first
sight, but this also is a region which should be seen in quietness
and peace, with time enough for the mind to feel the spell of
the place, and to respond to its influences of glad and soothing
repose. This part of the scenery of Niagara has peculiar attractions for thoughtful, earnest women, and is greatly enjoyed by
them. It might be said that feminine characteristics are predominant in the local qualities here, — in the brightness and free-
dom, and the gay, capricious motion which on every side invite
the eye, — and it is all brooded over by a spirit of deep and joyous
peace. At the Great Fall one feels the power of sterner, more
masculine elements, of massive strength and grandeur, and of
eternal, inexorable doom. The fateful element, the suggestion
of terror, the glad, unpitying play of resistless power, is, indeed,
everywhere present at Niagara, the fierceness of the tigress
under all the shrouding beauty, and making part of it; but this
is true of many kinds of beauty, and of some of the highest
things in human life, and the value and gladness of life are not
destroyed or lessened, but greatened thereby.

The beauty and charm of Niagara are not warm or sensuous
or tropical, but pure and bright and spiritual, belonging, as
already noted, to the realm of thought, and appealing to the

higher faculties of the soul of man. And this beauty and charm are not in the Falls alone, or even in the river alone. The interest and the value of the place depend even more upon the natural forest growth covering the islands and the banks of the river, the complex effect of the shrouding foliage, the solitudes thus created, and the natural shrines and sanctuaries of beauty, not yet marred and defiled by the hand of man, or desecrated by disfiguring buildings. If the trees on Goat Island and on all the smaller islands were cut down, and all the natural shrubbery and greenery destroyed, as it is probable will soon be done, the river would of course remain, and the waters would of necessity still pour over the precipice, as now. But Niagara would be destroyed beyond the possibility of restoration. All that now constitutes its peculiar charm, and its value as a source of quickening and life to the human spirit, all that now makes it a precious possession to the American people and to mankind, would have departed forever.

I am told that there are many people who do not understand this, because the truth and reason of the matter have never been presented to them. None of us know or understand such things until we learn them, until somebody teaches us their truth. If there are people who think that Niagara Falls would still be interesting, attractive, and valuable as a spectacle of grandeur and beauty, after the woods on the islands and riverbanks shall have been removed, and when wing-dams sprawl in every part of the American rapids, apportioning the drudging waters to their several race-ways and mill-wheels, — they are in error, through not fully understanding the matter, and by reason of not having sufficiently examined it. They would themselves, if these disfiguring changes should be accomplished, find Niagara entirely devoid of interest except in the direction of its commercial value, as a source of power for mills and factories. (This can as well be applied, and the water-power of the Niagara River can be utilized to any desired degree, without injury to the scenery about the Falls, but Goat Island is not the place for manufactures of any kind.)

If the business enterprises now contemplated are carried forward, Niagara will be one of the saddest, most painful scenes

on the globe to all thoughtful civilized men. They will behold
here the utter desolation and ruin of one of the fairest and
most precious possessions of the human race, the destruction by
our happy-go-lucky democracy of what should become one of
the chief sources of civilized enjoyment and spiritual delight to
the American people forever.

VII.

[*From the New York Tribune, Aug.* 29, 1882.]

DEFACEMENT OF SUBLIME SCENERY: THE COLORED-LIGHT
ABOMINATION — ROOKERIES AND RUBBISH-HEAPS — EVIL
EFFECT OF SUCH EXHIBITIONS ON PUBLIC MORALS —
THE CALL FOR PROMPT ACTION BY THE STATE.

NIAGARA FALLS, N. Y., Aug. 23, 1882.

THERE are some things at Niagara Falls which belong to the
lowest and worst world of which man knows anything; to a
world whose elements and influences are worse than wicked-
ness or positive wrong-doing, — the realm of ugliness and vulgarity, of influences which defile and befoul what is beautiful
and admirable, and so corrupt and poison the sources of life and
excellence. The tendency of friendly familiarity with ugliness
and vulgarity is to make the people not so much immoral as un-
moral; it leads to regions and conditions of life where the development of the moral sense, of the imagination, and of all high
qualities or faculties of the mind of man, is impossible. Nature's
Niagara is — or rather was — one of the grandest and loveliest
places on the globe. Some portions and features of this origi-
nal Niagara still remain, — enough of them to be well worth
preserving, — but they are, nearly all of them, likely soon to be
destroyed. Much of the natural loveliness, of the old charm,
of Niagara has already been obliterated and replaced by agencies and influences potent to vulgarize and debase the young
and untaught of the American people who for any reason visit
this spot which Nature made sacred to beauty and to all high
influences.

The best place to visit first, on arrival here, is the point at
the top of the American Fall on the "continental" side, that

is, nearest to the village. It is right and natural to begin
here, because the view from this point is more moderate,
or less striking and wonderful, than the view of the same fall
from Goat Island. It is the true place for the first view of
the Falls, and the scene, in its natural aspects, is indescribably
beautiful. One of America's foremost writers, whose works
have probably ministered a pure and wholesome delight to a
greater number of readers than those of any other American
author, tells us, in his history of a certain never-to-be-forgotten
journey to Niagara Falls, that as the visitors approached this
spot, they enjoyed, " at every instant, their feeling of arrival at
a sublime destination ; " and he adds, " In this sense Niagara
deserves almost to rank with Rome, the metropolis of history
and religion ; with Venice, the chief city of sentiment and fan-
tasy. In either you are at once made at home by a perception
of its greatness, in which there is no quality of aggression, as
there always seems to be in minor places, as well as in minor
men, and you gratefully accept its sublimity as a fact in no way
contrasting with your own insignificance."

Let me quote further, for I have a purpose : —

" In fact, that prodigious presence does make a solitude and silence
round every spirit worthy to perceive it, and it gives a kind of dignity
to all its belongings, so that the rocks and pebbles in the water's edge,
and the weeds and grasses that nod above it, have a value far beyond
that of such common things elsewhere. In all the aspects of Niagara
there seems a grave simplicity, which is perhaps a reflection of the
spectator's soul, for once utterly dismantled of affectation and con-
vention.

The last hues of sunset lingered in the mists that sprung from the
base of the Falls with a mournful, tremulous grace, and a movement
weird as the play of the Northern Lights. They were touched with
the most delicate purples and crimsons, that darkened to deep red,
and then faded from them at a second look, and they flew upward,
swiftly upward, like troops of pale, transparent ghosts ; while a per-
fectly clear radiance, better than any other for local color, dwelt upon
the scene. Far under the bridge the river smoothly ran, the under-
currents forever unfolding themselves upon the surface with a vast
roselike evolution, edged all round with faint lines of white, where
the air that filled the water freed itself in foam. What had been clear

green on the face of the cataract was here more like rich verd antique, and had a look of firmness almost like that of the stone itself. So it showed beneath the bridge, and down the river till the curving shores hid it. These, springing abruptly from the water's brink, and shagged with pine and cedar, displayed the tender verdure of grass and bushes intermingled with the dark evergreens that climb from ledge to ledge, till they point their speary tops above the crest of the bluffs. In front, where tumbled rocks and expanses of naked clay varied the gloomier and gayer green, sprung those spectral mists; and through them loomed out, in its manifold majesty, Niagara, with the seemingly immovable, white Gothic screen of the American Fall, and the green massive curve of the Horse-Shoe, solid and simple and calm as an Egyptian wall; while behind this, with their white and black expanses broken by dark-foliaged little isles, the steep Canadian rapids billowed down between their heavily wooded shores."

The last paragraph describes the view from the new suspension bridge, just below the Falls. These passages present, with the delicacy and accuracy possible to genius alone, a picture of the scene which is repeated almost every evening through weeks of fair summer weather every year. But now it is succeeded every night, almost before the sunset hues are fully withdrawn, by an indescribably painful and debasing exhibition. Electric lights are thrown through variously colored glasses, full upon "the white Gothic screen of the American Fall, and the green, massive curve of the Horse-Shoe." Blue and red and yellow rays are shot suddenly hither and thither upon the billowy rapids, and the boys who manage the lights amuse themselves by flashing their intolerable brilliance in the faces of people wherever they can be seen within range, and thus driving them from place to place to escape the blinding glare. When a red glass is used the American Fall has the appearance of the discharge-way of an enormous beet-sugar manufactory. When the yellowish glass is interposed the cataract looks much like the "tail-race" of an old-time wild-cat distillery on the Lower Maumee.

I was once riding on horseback near the Maumee River, in company with several Methodist ministers, when the wind brought to us very distinctly the odors from a distillery across the valley, half a mile away. The foremost man in the group

was a very earnest temperance advocate. As the scent reached
us he sniffed two or three times, then turned in the saddle, and
observed, "I smell hell." We have not this particular fragrance
at the Falls as yet, but even this may be here before many years
have passed, for one of the projects "for the development of the
resources of Niagara" talked of here is the erection of a mammoth distillery on Goat Island.

As things are now, the evening exhibition at the Falls on the
American side resembles the combination of a poor circus with
a cheap celebration of the Fourth of July. No description can
give to those who have not seen it an adequate notion of the
abominable effect of the colored electric lights when directed
upon the Falls. It is debasing, vulgarizing, and horrible in the
extreme. That children and young people should be exposed
to the influence of such a spectacle is matter for deepest regret
and sadness. It is evident that neither the people who make
this exhibition nor those who enjoy it would have any rooted
objection against the actual defilement of these crystal waters,
as their taste is actually so perverted that they have no joy in
their purity or beauty, but have a morbid and diseased pleasure
in their being made to look as if they were disgustingly be-
fouled and impure. Wordsworth's phrase, "vital feelings of
delight," is a most pregnant and suggestive expression; for there
are deadly feelings of delight as well as vital ones, and if young
people are not surrounded by beautiful and ennobling objects
and spectacles, many of them will come to delight in things
that are false, debasing, and monstrous. These evil influences
propagate themselves according to natural and universal laws,
and this exhibition of Niagara Falls in colors, by means of
electric lights, is a kind of evil missionary agency for the educa-
tion of the young people of America in the love of vulgarity
and ugliness. It is the fashion here to praise this exhibition as
something beautiful and "artistic," and it is often painful to
hear people talking such rubbish who ought to know better.
But it is always a little dull in the crowd of those who watch
the lights, and if anybody starts a conversation with a com-
panion many will listen, and, if propriety admits, as when a
general subject is discussed, will express agreement or approval.

After I had been here for some time this summer, being weary of hearing sensible-looking men and women say, "Oh, how beautiful!" and "Is n't that lovely?" I asked a gentleman at the hotel to go down with me one evening and help me try the effect of expressing dissent and dissatisfaction. He consented, and we were in the company at the parapet at Prospect Point when the red lights were turned on the beautiful cascade. We looked at it for a few moments, until the people around us began to talk, and then my friend observed earnestly that the exhibition. was in wretchedly bad taste, and tended to cheapen and degrade a sublime and noble spectacle, that it suggested a "variety" entertainment in a dance-hall in a mining town, and that it seemed as if the next thing should be the appearance of a girl in tights, with cymbals, to sing a comic song. I added that, as all the people had either seen the Falls during the day, or would do so on the morrow, it would be far better if we could quietly enjoy the beauty and wonder of the scene by the natural light of the moon and stars. We talked in this way for a few moments, and many persons near us expressed similar ideas and sentiments, and some even said, "Let us go; I do not care to look at that." As we walked back to the hotel the gentleman said, "I had seen it many times, but really I never thought before how ugly and unnatural it looked." Since then, as the company is mainly a new one each evening at the Point, we have repeated the experiment several times, with similar results. There is reason to believe that many people are influenced very considerably by the mere utterance and iteration of sentiments or opinions in their hearing, and in newspapers which they read; and as erroneous opinions and vicious tastes and influences are potent to propagate themselves by this means, it is very desirable that people who have knowledge and wholesome taste should also be ready to encourage adherence to high standards.

The press of the country can do much to bring about a better state of things at Niagara Falls. The predominant element in the existing state of things is the prevalence of ugliness, marring and neutralizing the nobility and harmony of a scene of wonderful natural grandeur and beauty. The colored-light nuisance is

but one feature, or instance, of this ugliness. Most of the structures in Prospect Park are obtrusively unbeautiful; but outside
of it, as one passes along the river front of the village, going up
the stream by the side of the American rapids, he encounters
such a variety or conglomeration of different kinds of ugliness
and slovenliness as is not often seen in a territory so contracted.
In a short walk one sees piles of lumber, heaps of sawdust and
of manure, scattered litter of scrap-iron and of many other
kinds of waste, old, unpainted, decaying buildings and sheds,
here the foundations of a house that has tumbled down, and
there a dirty area overgrown with rank, unsightly weeds. All
this, and much besides of similar repulsiveness, just where there
should be a walk shaded by beautiful trees, between the river
on one side and a forest belt on the other, which should shut
out the village from view.

But no real or considerable improvement is possible under
existing conditions of private land-ownership at Niagara. It
was a great and mischievous error — I fear a fatal mistake — to
allow the land adjacent to the Falls to become private property.
It should have been held forever by the State or by the National Government, in trust for the use and pleasure of the
people of our country. The only remedy which it now seems
possible to apply is the one suggested in the message of Governor Robinson (Jan. 9, 1879), and in a special report of the
Board of Commissioners of the State Survey, and the report of
the Director on the Preservation of the Scenery around Niagara
Falls. This report was transmitted to the Legislature of New
York March 22, 1880, by Horatio Seymour, President of the
Board. The commission was composed of the following distin-
guished gentlemen: W. A. Wheeler, Robert S. Hale, William
Dorsheimer, Francis A. Stout, George Geddes, and F. A. P.
Barnard. The report was made by Mr. James T. Gardner,
Director of the State Survey, and Mr. Frederick Law Olmsted.
It is a document of unusual interest and importance; and, what
is not always true of State reports or official documents, it
is wonderfully interesting and entertaining. It is a great pity
that it could not be published in some more popular form, and
so made accessible to the general public. It should be read in
every family in the State of New York.

It recommends the purchase, by the State of New York, of Goat Island and the smaller islands near it, and of the land on the American side of the river immediately contiguous to the Falls and to the rapids. By this means this invaluable national possession may be rescued from certain destruction. But whatever is done must be done speedily, or it will be too late. This would not be a great or difficult undertaking for the great State of New York. But American business men and leaders of society are usually ashamed or reluctant to acknowledge a real and practical interest in matters of taste. And yet every intelligent man knows that such agencies and influences are of great importance to national character. Those who understand the relation of material conditions to a high civilization ought to speak and act promptly and vigorously, in connection with this enterprise. I write of it in the hope that the press of the country may publish the facts widely, and discuss the subject thoroughly, with its usual intelligence, candor, and approval of all things good.

VIII.

[*From the Boston Daily Advertiser, Aug.* 18, 1882.]

MILLS AND MANUFACTORIES OCCUPYING THE SHORES AND
ISLANDS — THE BEAUTY OF THE AMERICAN SHORE AL-
READY DESTROYED — NECESSITY OF PROMPT ACTION TO
AVERT THE RUIN.

NIAGARA FALLS, N. Y., Aug. 14, 1882.

" CAN Niagara be saved? Is it worth while to try?" These
are among the questions which thoughtful and public-spirited
Americans ask, as they survey the difficulties which must be
overcome in order to make this great undertaking successful.
It is, of course, extremely difficult to obtain any considerable
attention for such an enterprise. The public mind is preoccupied. Politicians are, naturally and not unreasonably, reluctant
to concern themselves with matters not included in the scope or
issues of practical political affairs; and in this country almost
every man who can in any manner or degree influence public
opinion or action is a politician. Americans are a busy people,
and few of them have time or room for much thought or interest regarding anything outside of their daily work and business
interests. No wonder there seems little chance of bringing
many people to care about Niagara in time to prevent its destruction. But the public mind is always preoccupied, — always
has been, and always will be. And yet, in time past, public
attention has been awakened, and public interest secured, for
various matters which at first seemed to be outside of the range
of practical and necessary affairs; and such things will doubtless, from time to time, be done again. It is a very difficult
work, this of inducing the people of the country or of the State
of New York to hear, to read, to attend sufficiently to become
acquainted with the facts of the case, so that they can judge

intelligently of their importance. Perhaps it may require considerable time and much effort to accomplish this. But it can probably be done, and will be, I suppose, if a few men of character and ability come to feel how valuable are the interests which are imperilled here. Let us consider another class of obstacles or discouragements, which may be formulated or described in some such words as these: "The growth of wealth and of the selfish individualism which accompanies it (and which corrupts many who are not rich), seems to weaken all properly social motives and efforts. Men in cities and towns feel much less relation with their neighbors than of old. There is less civic patriotism; less sense of a spiritual and moral community. Though this is owing in part to other causes, it is mainly due to the selfishness of the individualism in a well-to-do democracy." There are great obstacles in the way of the effort to save Niagara from destruction; but I suppose our democracy can learn. It must, or it may not always be well-to-do. It may be that we cannot bring the mass of Americans to recognize any responsibility for the preservation of Niagara, or to feel any of the higher motives for doing so. If this should prove to be true, then the work would be not so much to save the Falls as to save our own souls. Were we to see the Falls destroyed without an effort to save them, the sin would be ours.

It is necessary to keep always clearly in mind the actual situation here. It may be very briefly described. It has three main features. 1st. The charm, interest, or value of Niagara is not in the river alone. The green foliage of the trees and vines on the shores and islands is an essential part of it, and if this natural framework of beauty is destroyed, the mere tumbling of the water over the precipice in a wilderness of mills and factories will yield no delight to any human being.

2d. The territory which is essential to the beauty and value of the scenery is being rapidly appropriated, and without some effectual interposition is likely soon to be all appropriated to industrial uses in the form of sites for mills and manufactories of various kinds. This is entirely unnecessary, because there are better sites far enough away from the Falls to leave the scenery undisturbed. But it is inevitable under the circum-

stances, because business interests demand it, the owners of the
land not being able to afford the luxury of such scenery, preserved and maintained at their private cost.

3d. All the evils which beset and the dangers which threaten
Niagara are the natural and necessary result of the private or
individual ownership of the lands contiguous to the river, and
are inseparable from it. So far as human judgment or foresight
can discover, the complete destruction of Niagara is certain to
be accomplished unless these lands can be converted from a
private possession into a public trust. Unless the State inter-
poses, Niagara will soon be a memory.

The beauty of the American shore of the river along nearly
the whole extent of the rapids has been entirely destroyed ; the
lovely growth of trees and swaying vines which formerly fringed
it, and overhung the rushing water, having been gradually removed. A long array of unsightly buildings (with heaps of
litter of various kinds) now takes the place of the ancient sylvan beauty. The same thing is true, essentially, of what was
once the most beautiful island in the American rapids. It is
occupied in part by a new paper-mill (which has a most piercing
and intolerable steam-whistle, which awakens every sleeper at
the nearer hotels), and in part by the desolation where an old
mill was burned down. In less than two years the youngest
heir to the estate of which Goat Island is a part will be of age,
and the island will then be sold. There is the strongest proba-
bility that, unless the State becomes the purchaser, it will be
bought for manufacturing purposes, and made the site of exten-
sive mills and shops. All the beauty of Niagara that now
remains unimpaired belongs to the islands, and this is the
fate that threatens it. Already wing-dams and ice-barriers
sprawl widely across what was the finest part of the American
rapids.

There are several classes of persons in this country who
should be most deeply concerned to avert this ruin. The
learned men who are specially interested in science, in its new
developments and broader applications, should not be silent
while Niagara is being destroyed by the commercial spirit
using science as its servitor. Shall science serve only the lower

practical and economic interests of human life? Are we to witness the complete ruin of this unique spectacle of natural beauty and grandeur without any remonstrance from the great teachers of science in this and other lands? Doubtless, when the destruction is accomplished, eloquent expressions of regret will not be wanting; but eloquence would be better employed in preventing the catastrophe than in bewailing it.

The educators of our country should be deeply interested. I suppose the colleges could save Niagara; certainly the men who have been trained in them could do so. It is highly gratifying and encouraging to thoughtful Americans to see the growing interest of our universities in classical learning and antiquities. It would be a misfortune and a shame not to sustain such work as that of the American Archæological Institute, for instance. Yet Niagara is worth more to the people of our country than the noblest temple that ever lifted its white front in the "pellucid air" of Greece. The intellectual conditions and atmosphere of a country that permits the destruction of Niagara cannot be expected to be favorable to high culture of any kind. It will be matter of interest to learn what is the feeling at Harvard, at Yale, at the University of Virginia, and in the colleges of the higher class generally in this country, regarding the interests imperilled here.

Our statesmen, who are interested in the higher aspects of national character and action, and who believe that democracy is specially suited to produce the most exalted and noble civilization, should not remain silent and indifferent while this evil threatens. Clergymen should be especially interested in the preservation of Niagara. The sentiments which it inspires, and the feelings which it nourishes, — the "vital feelings of delight" (to use Wordsworth's phrase of profound meaning) which are awakened here, — these influences are such as, in all times and lands, have been found especially favorable to religion and to all the higher activities and experiences of the spiritual nature of man. If there is any spectacle on earth which, more than any other, awakens what is deepest and best in the soul, filling it with adoring, reverent awe, that spectacle is Niagara. Will those whose special function it is to guard the higher spiritual interests of the nation see without concern the blotting out of this wonder of loveliness and grandeur?

But, far more than any particular or limited class, the common people of our country should feel interested in the preservation of Niagara. It is pre-eminently their possession, and if it is not destroyed, it is certain to be made more and more accessible and enjoyable to them. Whatever may be the measure of the influence and consequent responsibility of any of the classes which I have named, it is certain that here there is all necessary power. The people of New York can decree the preservation of Niagara. No doubt they would do so with all desirable promptness and emphasis, if the facts of the situation here could be plainly brought home to them. The revenues of a great and highly civilized people were never, in time of peace, used for a nobler object than this. The artists of the world, and all other lovers of natural beauty who have not seen Niagara, should visit it as soon as possible. In a very few years little may remain to suggest the once unparalleled glory and loveliness.

APPENDIX.

I.

[*From Harper's Weekly, Aug. 26, 1882.*]

THE RESCUE OF NIAGARA FALLS.

MORE than once we have spoken of the fatal injury done to the State of New York, and to the national character itself, by the desecration of Niagara Falls. In the letters of correspondents during this summer we have observed a complaint of the diminishing public interest in the Falls as a resort, and of the great falling off in the number of visitors. This is due to the total want of care in preserving the attractive character of the neighborhood. Every kind of disagreeable object is huddled along the shore, until the complete vulgarization of all the approaches and points of vantage, the nuisance of encroaching buildings and hackmen and Indian shops, and a multitude of petty annoyances, fairly repel the visitor, and give the worst of reputations for comfort and agreeability to a resort which should be among the most delightful in the country. When the immediate neighborhood of Niagara is covered with factories and tenement-houses and their dependencies, the sublime spectacle, one of the true wonders of the world, will be effectually and forever lost as an influence of moral elevation and happiness. And this fate is already impending. One of the islands has been already ruined as a part of the landscape; others are threatened. The bank all along the American rapids has been shorn of foliage, of trees and vines, and covered with mills, barns, sheds, and unsightly structures. In two years the

8

youngest heir of the Goat Island estate will come of age, and
the island will then be sold and covered with factories. This
is the time for action to save Niagara Falls. A few months
later, even, will be too late. Is it worth while to preserve this
natural wonder for the delight of the world? If it is, what
shall be done?

Niagara is a great water-power, and there is no need of losing
it as such. But that is not the question. It is not whether
Niagara is more valuable as factory power or as beauty and
sublimity, but how it shall best serve both use and beauty.
The answer is simple, for the situation is obvious. The river
above the Falls lies high over the lower country. Its power is
available everywhere. By drawing it off above the cataract,
and reserving a little space of shore, bank, and island all
around the Falls, the problem is solved: the factories are built
below; the cataract is saved. A strip of land broadening from
a hundred feet at the end to eight hundred or a thousand feet
above the Falls, inclosing the cataract and its immediate neighborhood, and capable of such landscape treatment as to plant
out every unsightly object, is all that is necessary. Such a plan
was suggested four or five years ago, and was most urgently
commended by leading men on both sides of the river. But it
was a general proposition, evidently most proper and desirable,
but involving expense and trouble. It was nobody's business
in particular, and after an admirable report from Mr. Olmsted, and some attempts to arouse public interest, the subject
dropped.

The representations now made, however, show that without
prompt action Niagara is lost, except as a water-power. The
rescue of the cataract, its proper preservation, and the permanent maintenance of its immediate vicinity as a public park,
is a duty which the State of New York may wisely undertake.
It is one of the public works for a high public purpose, like the
gift of statues of eminent New-Yorkers to the Capitol at Wash-
ington, which public opinion would undoubtedly authorize.
There is no doubt that if a few active, intelligent, and interested
men in the State should take the project in hand upon the general basis of Mr. Olmsted's report, inviting him to make such

further suggestions as might occur, the work would be done. Suitable representations to the Governor and general discussion in the press would unquestionably procure a recommendation to the Legislature, which would find then a responsive public spirit, so that it would be seed sown in a fruitful soil. Let New York spare herself the shame of the practical obliteration of Niagara Falls.

II.

[From a Letter in the New York Herald, Sept. 9, 1882.]

COLUMBUS, OHIO, Sept. 6, 1882.

Is there not throughout the State of New York a general apathy toward this great improvement which intelligent discussion and patriotic appeal alone can overcome? Such measures as free canals, a new aqueduct or new park for New York City, may appear as more practical and pressing wants. Yet, sorely needed as those things are, it is yet true that if the Niagara reform were fairly considered on the length and breadth of its merits, its importance would appear even higher and greater than any other need of the State. This transcendent gift of nature must be restored and reconsecrated to the high uses of its own sublimity and beauty. This must be done in the interest of the State, of the nation, and of travellers from every clime and country. Not another year should pass without finding this work well in hand.

There has been considerable desultory writing upon this subject, inadequate, however, to produce much effect. A vigorous general discussion in the press would greatly aid in making clear the urgency of the movement. It would arouse the interest of the many thousand citizens who possess sufficient culture to perceive the priceless value and utility of such imperial grandeur for its own sake. A State that can, without serious opposition, squander more millions upon its Capitol than the United States have expended upon theirs, will not, when it comes to the sticking point, begrudge a million or two to save Niagara. Niagara is a beautiful name, and it stands for a scene which, from the days of Father Hennepin, has been an object of wonder and delight, almost of worship, to pilgrims from every portion of the globe. Will you not for the public good renew the agitation of this question with some such energy and good effect as that with which you are now urging a wise selection for the next State Executive? To permit the beggarly crew of millers, paper-makers, sawyers, showmen, and the vermin of small venders who now infest Niagara's brink to go on and complete their work of destruction, as they surely will unless thrust out by the strong arm of the State, were a folly and madness compared to which the burning of the Louvre by the Commune were an act of supreme wisdom. Even the Louvre might in time be restored; but, once destroyed, who shall restore thee, Niagara, thou "cunningest pattern of most excelling Nature"? Let the defilers of this temple of divine beauty be driven out with the scourge of law and righteous indignation.

III.

[From the New York Tribune, Sept. 12, 1882.]

NIAGARA — A SUGGESTION.

THE Marquis of Lorne, it is stated, favors the scheme of the International Park at Niagara, and will probably take steps to forward it. But what can Lord Lorne do in the premises? It is not the Canadian side of the Falls that is disgraced with gigantic factories, or penny schemes of cheating, or tawdry electric lights. Practically the Canadians have left the great Fall to Nature. Every American of decent feeling, or the slightest regard for propriety even, agrees with the Marquis in this matter. That the owners of the property think differently is a pity, but not perhaps to be wondered at. It is a matter with them mainly of taste, and of luxury and comfort for themselves and their children during life. If the whole American nation, which professes to be outraged by the vulgar desecration of this wonder of Nature, cannot afford to buy it and keep it free from desecration, why should two or three individuals bear the whole burden ? A dollar apiece from the wealthy men of two or three of our large cities would save the country from the disgrace of turning Niagara into a great natural engine for paper-mills and washing-tub factories ; and so long as they do not give it, how can they ask the Smiths or Joneses, whose whole property is this Fall, to sacrifice their entire substance ?

There has been a good deal of vague talk about this International Park. Meetings have been held, and influential men have declared themselves boldly in favor of it. But there the matter has stopped. Why ? Is it that we do not see how urgent the need of action is ? No American can go to Niagara without feeling his face burn with shame. Vulgarity, pretension, a trading spirit of the very lowest kind, have taken possession of this most sublime gift of Nature to us. It gives a character to the nation in the eyes of foreigners, a character which we actually do not deserve. If neither Congress nor the State of New York will move in the matter, why do not the women of America ? They saved Mount Vernon, by a little steady, persistent effort, to be a sacred possession for us for all time. Why can they not save Niagara ?

IV.

[*From the Nation, Sept.* 14, 1882.]

THE " Tribune " calls upon the women of America, who "saved Mount Vernon," to unite in a movement to save Niagara and keep it free from the vulgar desecration from which it is now suffering. It says: " If neither Congress nor the State of New York will move in the matter, why do not the women of America?" There is a fundamental difference between the case of Mount Vernon and that of Niagara which the " Tribune " seems to have overlooked. The interest in Mount Vernon is due to historical, political, and patriotic causes, and was widespread. The amount of money, too, required was very small. But the work of saving a waterfall from desecration involves an appeal to the love of the beautiful, — a sentiment much less strong in the United States than some other sentiments. Governor Cornell probably fairly represents the feeling of the average American man as to Niagara, and his observation, on hearing of the movement for an international park, was an inquiry as to whether the defeat of the scheme would prevent the water from coming over the falls. There is no doubt, however, that for the American woman the beautiful possesses a deeper interest than for the American man, and if she can be roused to do something for Niagara, there is no telling what she may accomplish. A good deal has been made of the violent opposition of the hackmen, guides, and other waterfall parasites who now make money out of the *laissez-faire* system prevailing at Niagara. But this has been a good deal overestimated. It is indifference which is at the root of the trouble.

www.ingramcontent.com/pod-product-compliance
Lightning Source LLC
Chambersburg PA
CBHW021228260626
47172CB00002B/662